My Life with the Wave

to Judit Bodnar
— CC

to the Gish family,
with special thanks to Carol and Griffin
— MB

This story is based on "My Life with the Wave," included in *Eagle or Sun? (¿Aguila o sol?)*,
Published by New Directions Publishing Corporation. Used by permission.
Copyright © 1960 by Fondo de Cultura Economica.

Acrylic and oil paints were used for the full-color illustrations. The text type is 16-point Fenice.

My Life with the Wave
Text copyright © 1997 by Catherine Cowan
Illustrations copyright © 1997 by Mark Buehner
Manufactured in China by South China Printing Company Ltd.
All rights reserved.
www.harperchildrens.com
Library of Congress Cataloging-in-Publication Data
Cowan, Catherine.
My life with the wave / by Octavio Paz ; as retold for children by Catherine Cowan :
illustrated by Mark Buehner.
p. cm.
Summary: A child befriends a wave at the seashore and brings her home.
ISBN 0-688-12660-X (trade) — ISBN 0-688-12661-8 (lib. bdg.)
ISBN 0-06-056200-5 (pbk.)
[1. Ocean waves—Fiction. 2. Friendship—Fiction.] I. Paz, Octavio. II. Buehner, Mark, ill. III. Title.
PZ7.C8347My 1994   93-33625
[Fic]—dc20   CIP
                                                                                  AC

My Life with the Wave

Based on the story by
OCTAVIO PAZ

Translated and adapted for children by
CATHERINE COWAN

Illustrated by
MARK BUEHNER

HarperCollinsPublishers

My first trip to the seashore, I fell in love with the waves. Just as we were about to leave, one wave tore away from the sea. When the others tried to stop her by clutching at her floating skirts, she caught my hand, and we raced away together across the wrinkled sand.

My father tried to send her back, but
the wave cried and begged and threatened
until he agreed that she could come along.

The next morning we went to the station and boarded the train. The wave was tall and fair and full of light—she was bound to attract attention. If there was a rule forbidding waves from traveling by train, the conductor might throw her off. So, cup by small cup, when no one was looking, I emptied the watercooler, and she hid herself inside it.

When we arrived home, the wave rushed into our house....

Before, she had been one wave; now, she was many. She flooded our rooms with light and air, driving away the shadows with her blue and green reflections. Small forgotten corners crowded with dust and dark were swept by her light. The whole house shone with her laughter. Her smile was everywhere.

The sun came into our old, dark rooms and stayed for hours and hours. It loved dancing with the wave and me so much that it sometimes forgot to leave. More than once it crept out through my window as the stars watched in amazement.

The wave and I played together constantly. If I caught and hugged her, she would rise up tall like a liquid tree, then burst into a shower and bathe me in her foam. If I ran at her and she stood still, I would find myself wrapped in her arms. She would lift me up, then let me fall, only to catch me and lower me to the floor as gently as a feather.

At night we lay side by side, whispering secrets with smiles and smothered laughter. She rocked me to sleep in her waters and sang sweet sea songs into the shell of my ear. Sometimes in the dark she shimmered like a rainbow. To touch her then was like touching a piece of night tattooed with fire.

Other nights she was black and bitter. In dark despair she howled and sighed and twisted. Hearing her, the sea wind came flying over the mountains. It wailed with a wild wind voice through the trees and clawed all night at my windows.

Cloudy days enraged the wave. She smashed my model train, soaked my stamp collection, and covered my room in her gray and greenish foam....

She was pulled by the moon, the sun, and the stars: Her moods were as changeable as the tide.

I thought she might be lonely and gave her seashells and a tiny sailboat to play with. After she smashed these against the wall, I brought home small fish for her. She swept them into her arms, then whispered and played with them by the hour. At night, while she slept, the fish adorned her hair with little flashes and splashes of color.

Finally I grew angry. Now the wave spent all her time playing with the fish and never played with me. I tried to catch them, but they darted like ghosts between my fingers while the wave poured over me in foaming laughter.

With the coming of winter, the sky turned gray and the city shivered, drenched in a frozen rain. The wave had nightmares. She dreamed strange dreams of the icy regions of the poles, of turning to ice and sailing away to where the nights go on for years. She curled herself into a corner and howled through long, long days and longer nights. She filled the house with phantoms and called up monsters from the deep....

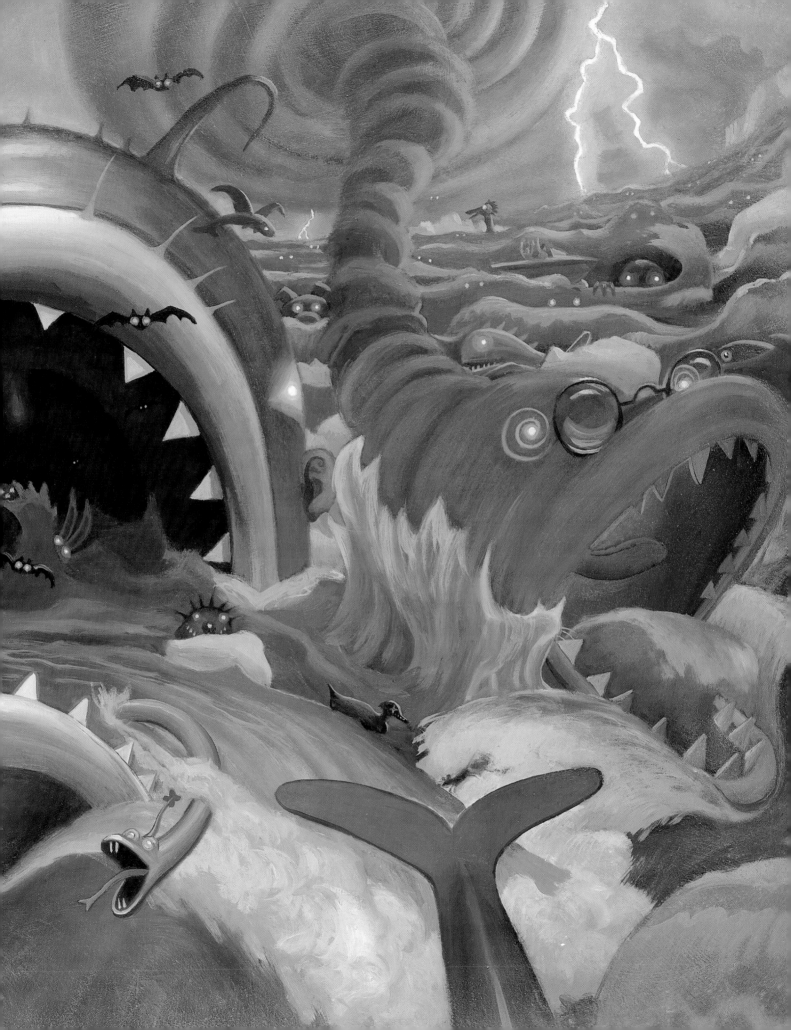

My father said she would have to go.
My poor mother was nearly crazy. Since
I could never catch the wave, we packed
and went away for a time, leaving her
behind in the cold.

When we returned, we found the wave frozen—a beautiful statue of ice. Though it broke my heart, I helped my father wrap her in a quilt, and we carried her back to the sea.

Now the house is dark again, and the corners are filled with dust and shadows. Sometimes I lie awake at night and remember. My parents say good riddance to bad waves and I am never to bring home another. But I miss my friend.

Maybe next year, if we go to the mountains, I'll bring home a cloud. Clouds are soft and cuddly and would never act like a wave.